How the Ministry of Fun Came to Be!

LiLi Townsend

It's High Fun for me to share my mystical adventure stories with you. They are a way that we can ALL share our awakenings. I love to ask friends to tell, and feel as they do, what stirred them and eventually brought them to this precious

Here and Now!

So, sit back in your comfy Soul Selves, and observe the unfolding of this soul/ego's experience with love, compassion, and humor... Divine humor!

~LiLi

The Evolution

"Hey! Where's the Minister of Fun?
There are some folks here who are
ready to be ordained!"

. . . . . And, here I am walking towards
the stage with anxious anticipation
and delight! Who would have thought
that my adventure path would lead
me to this; a roomful of people
choosing to take themselves Lightly!

Life is a Mystery School! Each one of
Us is a Mystery School! There are
over seven billion Beings here on
Earth, and each one unique. Isn't that
a miracle in itself? And each one as
complicated as I am.

My Mystery School began in a sophisticated New York with the eternal questions of soul-searching penetrating through the veneer of a fascinating but spiritually empty life. Who am I? What are we all doing here? What's the point of this existence? Marijuana had opened my mental gates of curiosity and made me grateful for my life in a new and deeper way.

It was the 70's, and I began to see that my successful career in fashion and the arts, and my marriage to a charming alcoholic man were leading into a death spiral of champagne, cocaine, and shallow frivolity. It was empty. My big career was completely meaningless. I had to bust loose for myself and for my teenage son. The life I was leading set no example for him and no future for me. It was time for my beloved son to live with his father. It was time for a more stable life with his Dad, difficult as that turned out to be.

I left New York, maintaining a wee toehold, an apartment called the LiLipad. I was headed on an adventure, questing into the unknown. In a series of synchronicities, I was invited to sail with a delightful architect throughout the Caribbean. I landed on a little, strong, and scrappy oceangoing ketch called "Venus." I had learned to sail at a yacht club on Long Island Sound. I had always yearned for deep-water sailing. We were seafaring for days without a landfall, and I spent many nights at the helm, alone on a four-hour watch, while my skipper slept.

On those lone nights I experienced a deep solitude under the vast starry skies; calm nights of peaceful pondering. I felt connected to the Universe, sensing an innate knowing beyond the confines of man-made religious thought, for which I had both reverence and contempt.

Miles from land, I felt a naturalness of Being, a new joy. There were nights of terror too. Stormy nights with towering waves challenged my fears. Desperate prayers for safety came from deep within my small scared self. "Oh God help me! Please save us in this tiny boat in your vast ocean.

Help! Help!" Then at last, a warm peace would penetrate my whole Being, the fear blooming into excitement. "Whoow!" Surfing down the waves, the sturdy "Venus" felt agile and light. It was thrilling as the surging ocean lifted the boat past each dangerous cresting wave. "This is the edge! "Whee!" I shouted. "I love this! I am brave and I am fearless! Yippee!" I felt a new closeness and trust for the Divine Intelligence, a personal sense of connection.

The Skipper and I had an introvert/extrovert relationship, which buoyed us for two years of affection, adventure, and camaraderie. We met other people living on boats, raising families, sharing sailing stories and meeting up in exotic ports. We befriended an array of characters from one end of the Caribbean to the other. The mundane realities of boat maintenance interspersed with exploring different islands kept us busy and content.

The burning questions persisted, aided by whatever spiritual books I could find along the way. The concept of the unity of body, mind and spirit seemed to be coming up frequently, propelling me out of the boat life and into the unfolding New Age world.

Now in the 80's, my Mystery School Curriculum burgeoned with holistic healing, massage, acupuncture, Reiki, nutrition, Sufi poetry, Buddhist thought, and expanding wonder. I became a workshop junkie attending conferences on the environment, indigenous wisdom and meditation, shamanism and trust exercises, like walking on hot coals. And always, I found profound teachers along the way. Years of study, travel, and being, guided by my inner knowing, convinced me of an important lesson: I am always HOME! My spiritual life was deepening. A counselor training helped me to focus on healing others as well. I learned that we all have healing hands. Using them in my sessions brought a rich feeling of fulfillment. The work evolved into a process called Genealogical Clearing. I loved it!

One day, at a sailing event in Newport, Rhode Island, I met my childhood crush who had been an older boy at sailing school. He had matured into a tall handsome man with a long sensitive face and intelligent humor in his gray blue eyes. It seemed destiny was calling.

"Is this the man of my dreams? I wondered, "Let's see how it grows." And grow it did. It was a long-distance romance between New York and San Francisco. Magical meetings over a year blossomed into warm expectancy. I dared to imagine a future on the West Coast, exploring an edge of possibility with Alan. We planned to sail on different boats in the Bermuda Race, a high point in any sailor's life. We also planned to

train with our crews for a romantic
week and then start for Bermuda and
a new phase of our lives. My son was
to fly to Bermuda and meet Alan for
the first time.

NOTHING could have prepared me
for what came next.

Alan died! Admitted for a sore throat
with a non-fatal disease called
Quinsy's, Alan was given the wrong
injection and died in a San Francisco
hospital. He was 48 years old.

My heart blew open into a million
shards. Grief and rage tore me to
shreds. I wailed and whimpered,
picturing Alan's last hours.
Was he suffering? Was he in pain? Did
he know what was happening to him?

Was this going to be my dark night of the soul? How could I find my way out or through this painful place?

We shared a touching classic love song called, "I Remember You." A note was found at his bedside; he had written out the last verse:

"When my life is through,
And the angels ask me to recall,
The thrill of them all,
Well, I will tell them,
I remember You."

My stiff upper lip, which had carried me through two divorces, disappointments and betrayal, had vanished in an instant. Life was forever changed.

I always felt that Alan and I had a sacred soul contract. That somehow his kismet, his timing for leaving this plane, would crack my heart OPEN. My heart remains open, and I am grateful forever.

Shift

I knew it was time for another huge
shift. I wanted a fresh start. In my
heart, I had already left the city life in
New York, and I wanted to follow the
faint signs to what was next. I had
lived in Aspen for my Counselor
training and fell in love with the Rocky
Mountains, which ended in the
oceanic plains of New Mexico. I was
drawn to the allure of Santa Fe, a
spiritual crossroads of many cultures.

Santa Fe

In the first two months, I was blessed to stay with new friends who lived north of Santa Fe, in a tiny hamlet called Tesuque. My hostess, Lynn, was a savvy and sassy artist, and her husband, Claude, was a brilliant physicist from Los Alamos. Our quantum physics and mystical conversations lasted long into the starlit nights and set the tone for my inner explorations as well as the outer ones.

"Let's go hiking in Bandolier State Park today," said Lynn enthusiastically. "I want you to see the ruins, they will blow you away!"

"Oh, I really should go house hunting today, don't you think?" I replied.

"No worries, love," Lynn countered. "I have a funny feeling that with your luck a perfect place is already waiting for you. Let's Go!"

Lynn, with her athletic bod, kitted out in walking shorts and a sun proof shirt, wasn't taking "No" for an answer. My surrender came easily since the high desert terrain already enchanted me.

"Tell me about the Anasazi people who lived here." I asked.

"Well, first of all, we don't use the term 'Anasazi' anymore. It is a deep insult.

The Navajos used it to slime the Ancestral Puebloan people.

"Really, why would they do that?" I wondered.

Lynn's dark eyes flashed with indignation, "Politics, of course. Even back then all the tribes sought favor with the Bureau of Land Management by fair means and foul. There was a lot of foul coming at the Natives from many directions. Shameful really."

"It seems these cultural relations were very complex." I ventured.

"Yes, the Navajos came from the North, they were peaceful, but pushy. They just kept moving into Hopi territory and succeeded because there was no pushback from the Tewa and Hopi people. The Hopi Elders just wanted peace to carry on their ancient mission of keeping the world in balance."

Across the plains studded with mesquite and pine, we admired the powerful silhouettes of Black Mesa, while Lynn continued to intrigue me with history. The fantastical sandstone conical spires towered above the meandering Rio Grande, while feathery willow and cottonwood softened the edges.

Tears

Absorbed in the beauty of nature, the aliveness pulsing all around me, I felt a wave of longing pass through me, the recurring "what if, what ifs" wrung my heart again. "It's so beautiful," I murmured, tears gently flowing down my cheeks. "I'm so sad that I couldn't share this with Alan."

"I understand. So, how's your heart feeling today?" Lynn asked softly.

"I feel quite tender…sort of raw. I can't help but think of the dream we shared of prowling around these parts. Alan loved Georgia O'Keefe's work, and we wanted to visit her studio just a few miles up from here and beyond that, the Ghost Ranch, too."

"I get it. Georgia is the legend of here. This is the perfect place to grieve that, Honey. Just let it be. Beauty herself heals. Remember Leonard Cohen's song, "Hallelujah"? He says, 'It's the crack. It's the crack in everything that lets the Light come in!'"

"Well, I've got the crack going on, now where's the light?" I quipped.

"Have you ever heard of Hakomi?"

"Nope, what's that?"

"Body centered psychotherapy. Taking cues from what your body is feeling at the moment and using emotional intelligence to get at core materials," explained Lynn.

"I know a highly qualified practitioner, Sharon. I feel she would be helpful in getting down to the bare bones of your grief and anything else that is lurking in your history."
"Sounds like a plan," I whispered.
"My chest and gut feel like I've been cow-kicked. All the breath knocked out of me. I am so ready to shift all this pain." This was the beginning of several years of profound healing.

Sharon's insightful and intuitive work was lifesaving and life giving. Each week another layer of sorrow lifted while we explored back to childhood wounds gently releasing hurts and

unexplored depths. She helped me
be present to all aspects of my life.
She helped me to see the weaving of
events as perfect steps on my path
leading to evolution and
transformation.

She offered wise counsel: "Yes, your
heart has been torn open and your
Being is tender. You have chosen to
work and transmit energy to others in
the name of Great Spirit. To know
this path, you must have been truly
wounded. You must know what pain
is. You must be able to empathize in
the deepest way with people who are
suffering."

I continued my healing with
acupuncture and Rolfing. Hiking and
bathing in the healing waters of Ojo

Caliente, a natural hot spring in
northern New Mexico, and making
new friends. Gradually, I cleared
body, mind and Spirit. A contented
joy opened me to the charms of new
people, art, meditation, and
exploration.

I walked in the red canyons and
arroyos accompanied by raucous
and chatty crows. I found favorite
perches for dreamily conversing with
my inner presence. In the calm
beauty, the voice seemed more
audible and available than ever
before. On my colorful Pendleton
blanket under a shady grove of
cottonwood trees, I breathed myself
into a beautiful space of feeling
radically alive. I offered prayers of

gratitude to Earth Mother, the
sacred land and Sky Father.

A Cherokee/Comanche Wiseman had
fascinated me with the stories of his
elders and the deep wisdom and
magic that they shared. It was
nourishing to feel part of the living
land, the rock formations, the
bristling piñon trees and understand
that humans, ancestors and families
had walked this land for ages past.
John Freesoul taught me to lose
myself by shaking my rattle and
watching colors and patterns forming
behind my closed eyes, honoring
those who had come before.

"Oh, dear God, thank you for lifting
this veil of sorrow. Thank you for
helping me discover old wounds from

the past, lost loves, betrayals and all the unhappiness that has been lodged in my heart and in my gut for so long. I feel that now is the time to heal all the fear and sadness in my past. I call upon my angels, guides, and my deepest Soul to help me now!"

I was rebuilding from the inside out. I saw my heart as a receiver of Divine energy, a strong receiver that was mending and growing in the Land of Enchantment. I pledged myself to Earth Mother and to her healing with the emerging environmental movement.

Soon, by a series of heartful connections with new friends, I was given an opportunity to rent a beautiful old adobe. It was eccentrically furnished on Camino del Monte Sol, in the old part of Santa Fe, and a welcoming oasis for us all. I became entranced by the culture of the Native people and the changing art scene. I felt settled and happy!

To Egypt~

My mystical curriculum continued with
a fascination for the Egyptian
Mysteries, the Emerald Tablets of
Thoth, God of the Moon, magic and
writing. It described the ancient
wisdom teachings of the Children of
Light, coming perhaps from as far
back as Atlantis. Thoth says,

"For only in the search for truth
could my soul be stilled
And the flame within me quenched."

The tablets spoke of waves of
consciousness coming to help the
people grow upwards in Soul Force.
It said,

"Lie in the sarcophagus of stone in my chamber, then I will Reveal to him the Great Mysteries. Lift ever upwards your eyes to the Light."

The Invitation

"Good afternoon," said a rather stately voice, "May I please speak to Maude?"

"Oh, so sorry," I said. "Maude left two days ago".

"That's a pity. I know that she loves the Egyptian mysteries, and I planned to invite her to Egypt."

"Interesting! Well, I too am studying them," I countered.

"Are you really? I'm taking a group of metaphysicians for 17 days of touring the sacred sites and working with the ancient texts. We will have daily meditations as well," said John Thomas.

I could hardly believe it! My heart began to pound with excitement. "Yes," continued John, "Please join us. We'll be sailing up the Nile, coordinating our trip to include a full moon eclipse over the Temples at Karnak."

My Mum, Elsita, and I had been considering a trip for years. Elsita had been in Egypt in 1922, at the height of the hubbub when King Tut's tomb was opened, and she always longed to return. This seemed a heaven-sent opportunity! How could we refuse! And so, we went!

We stayed in the very same hotel, the Mena House. Opulent and exotic, it overlooked the pyramids on the Plains of Giza. The Sphinx loomed majestically nearby. Our group of six dined and celebrated in the famous old hotel, and that night, that fateful night, I drank an iced drink with a dose of what I called "Ramses Revenge." For days I suffered and purged and eventually lightened myself right up!

Nothing could dampen our delight as we viewed dusty Cairo and the colorful sights and sounds of the Bazaar—fabrics shot with threads of silver, the fragrance of jasmine and rose, embroidered slippers and sacred amulets with magical properties We arrayed ourselves with long cotton djebellahs to keep us cool-ish in the fierce heat. We prowled the historical antiquities in the Cairo Museum in wonder, with

King Tut's treasure displayed in its dazzling magnificence.

A graceful felucca, with its huge sail aloft, took us to the legendary island of Philae, where Queen Isis took refuge after her King, Osiris was murdered by his brother, Set. We learned and reveled in the dramatic history of the Pharaohs.
We set off on a week long cruise up the Nile, where we joined a group of 20 metaphysicians from Power Places Tours. They had a historian with them who shared the Meta history that pushed the dates back beyond what is commonly taught. He strangely resembled a historical figure, Bes, who was a court jester, priest and wise man. We visited the Valley of the Kings and Queen

Hatshepsut's vast temple complex. We visited the Aswan Dam, with its colossal pharaonic statues that had been rescued and elevated above the dam's waterline.

We anchored at Karnak, before the Avenue of the 80 Sphinxes, where we watched in awe at the full moon eclipse. The orange moon looked like a three-dimensional pumpkin in the star strewn night sky.

Mum offered up a prayer:

"Oh Mother-Father God,
In this moment of awesome beauty,
we pray for our planet, which we love
but which, in our ignorance we have
so badly treated. Please help us
restore its purity and integrity so that
its waters, from which we rose, may
again sparkle like crystal, its oceans,
lakes and rivers may flow in clarity
and the fishes, whales, and dolphins
that inhabit them may rejoice."

"Help us to purify the air over our
heads and the earth under our feet,
so that the planet may be green and
wholesome and the woods and
jungles flourish, so that the birds of
the sky and the beasts of the field
may again be healthy and the
creatures of the forest find shelter
and multiply."

"Above all, may the hearts of men be purified, so that the misunderstandings that have divided us may disappear and the Most Great Peace may come to pass."

And as we prayed, Earth's shadow, which had darkened the face of the moon, moved away and she was revealed in all her glory.

AMEN

In the Stars

"Stars! Millions of stars before me in every direction! Towards the left I could see ... STARS. Gazing ahead, a myriad of stars, against the blue hub of heaven, lit the sky. I have the knowing that everything is possible. I can move in any direction; any way I choose will be perfect. I am at peace with a sense of expectancy. My gaze sweeps to the right, it's filled with swaths of tiny lights. Then, far right below me is a blue star. A shock! "It's Earth! Oh my God! I have a whole life down there!" I felt myself swoop down in that direction and instantly opened my eyes to greet the twenty-five people who surrounded the cool granite sarcophagus where I am lying. Blinking into the low light of the

King's Chamber in the Great Pyramid,
I take my place in the circle while the
next metaphysician climbs into the
sarcophagus. I hear the chanting of
OM and RA and the strange
boomeranging sound, 'waowaowao',
which penetrates our awareness.

"Holy Smokes! I was out in space with
my full consciousness and no body! I
didn't need a body! I was complete
and safe and whole, and it all felt so
alive!"

Just minutes ago, we were trudging
up the musty narrow steps leading up
to the King and Queen's chambers.
Twenty-six souls were traveling to
investigate the mysteries of Egypt,
each called by a longing to
understand the profound questions

of who we are and why we are here. And, what the Egyptian cosmology has to do with it and if that connects with ancient Hawaiian histories.

It was two days before I could share my experience with our small group of six at our daily meditation. I felt shy to present my truth, but I relived those moments and the astonishing feeling of Oneness and naturalness in my heart. I was finally able to speak of the wonder I was still feeling. My companions, including Elsita, were as stunned as I had been. Our leader, John, said, "You must have been in the Egyptian Mystery School, which required initiates to learn to leave their bodies and fly out the top of the pyramid."

"But," I reasoned, "I must have exited from the side since Earth was below me on my right." Later, when we checked a diagram of Khufu's pyramid, we saw two diagonal channels slanting out from the chamber. It was stated that they were intended as exits for the king's soul. I felt overjoyed to know in my being that consciousness does not need a body to exist. I no longer needed to fear the extinguishment of Death.

Life was forever changed!

Rome? Paris? Or London?

What next after Egypt? I was figuring
out our route map when a photo-
postcard arrived from a dear and
esteemed friend, Peter, who was
standing in front of a castle-like
structure called The Tor of
Glastonbury. His words were, "Still
high in high places!" What timing!

I had just finished reading an
enchanting book called, "The Mists
of Avalon" about the waning days of
the pagan cultures and the overlay of
Christianity in the Roman era of
Briton. I had adored the book by
Marion Bradley and the legendary
times of King Arthur's Court as
viewed from the feminine perspective
of Morgan Le Fey and the Lady of

the Lake. The story had centered on Glastonbury. Bingo! I booked us into the U.K.

We reveled for a few days in the civilization and delights of London before driving on a cross-country trip to the South West, to Somerset. One curiosity occurred on the way. We were riding in a traditional boxy London cab when I spotted a small bible on the seat. I moved to hand it to the driver when my inner voice said, *"This is for you."* Since I never before had owned a bible, I was a bit surprised, but tucked it into my traveling bag.

We were thrilled to behold the towering Stonehenge, the ancient stones and a famous focal point for early rituals. We were honored to witness a ceremony of cloaked Druids raising their mighty prayers as ever, across time.

From afar, as we approached, we could see the crenellated single tower rising from the summit of a rounded slope, the highest spot in Avalon, The Tor of Glastonbury. We drove into the charming town to find our B&B on a quiet side street. It was cozy and remarkable for a mural of a great tree with splendid roots and a complex trunk, which climbed through the house to flourish on the top floor. We drove down a leafy hedgerow to park on a lane where sunlight filtered through the greenery. After parking close to the grassy dome of St. Michael's hill, we

climbed the pale limestone path,
which sloped up to the Tor. Tawny
sheep grazed keeping the turf neatly
trimmed. A dark bluestone tower is all
that remains of a monk's dwelling
place and monastery dedicated to
the Archangel Michael. The wrath
and whim of King Henry the VIII and
his henchman, Oliver Cromwell,
destroyed the buildings.
The vista before us revealed hamlets
and streams and lakes punctuated by
the steeples of nearby towns. I fell
into a reverie as the sun set in a
glorious riot of color.

It seemed a dream to be here
overlooking what was once a shallow
inland sea, with hilly mounds rising
above waters. "These are the Mists

of Avalon!" I exulted. "Worshippers have gathered here at this magical place across the spread of history!.And I am here!" My inner voice clearly stated, *Come back by yourself before sunrise!*

I vowed to do so without question. I set my alarm for 4 a.m. and feeling quite safe and natural, made my way through the cobblestoned streets and quaint buildings. When I reached the brow of the hill, I was surprised to see a man in a red slicker.

"Are you going up to the Tor?" he asked kindly.
"Yes I am. Am I on the right path?"
"I think you'd prefer the proper front way. Just turn left on the lane ahead."

"Very kind, thank you."
"Have a lovely night," he said, as he
tipped his hat.

The path was very open, revealing a
dark starry sky. I felt such joy as I
walked along with Sirius and the
constellation of Orion's belt
overhead. A chill breeze invigorated
my walk as I reflected upon the
events in Egypt. I felt that my inner
feminine had been healed by the
study of Isis and the women's
mysteries and by the spectacular
journey from the King's Chamber into
the unknown, but somehow
comforting realms.

As I approached the casual wooden
opening to the pathway, I suddenly
felt that a barrier of cold fear barred

my way. I stood, rooted to the spot, and said, out loud "What is this? I cannot cross this threshold." I waited for my inner voice to guide me. Nothing. "I thought you wanted me to be here!" Nothing. I finally realized that I needed to take action myself. I whipped out a small plastic kid's wand, filled with plastic stars, "Isis! Help me!"

I strode forward, feet firmly marching up the spiraling path. I still felt the heaviness of fear all around me. It was incomprehensible. I wondered if there might be lost souls there where so many monks had been killed. It wasn't logical, but I prayed and cried all the way to the top of the rounded hill. Finally reaching level ground – Poof! I felt that I'd exploded like a

champagne cork flying out of a
bottle. I started to laugh with relief
and dance with abandon. I thought to
myself, *You are such a pagan!* and
laughed heartily as I twirled. I glanced
up at the imposing tower. It seemed
so phallic, and I recognized that my
inner male must have been healed,
too. I danced waving my arms in a
figure eight pattern of balance. I felt
whole as never before!

After a while, feeling chilled, I entered
the Tor; the bluestone walls open on
two sides. Being a proper New Ager, I
had feathers and crystals in my
pockets for my small altar. I was
shivering with cold in the December
night.

After a while, I began to feel warmth at the back of my neck. Oh, it felt so good to feel the heat traveling across my shoulders and down my spine and arms. It felt as if my spine was somehow electrified. Eventually I said to myself in wonder, *Oh, there must be an angel or something BIG here.* In a flash I somehow intuited that it was Christ consciousness. "Well," I firmly announced, "I've never had anything to do with you!" In the silence the inner awareness spoke, "*You have not chosen me, but I have chosen you! And, I ordain you now to be my minister.*" "A minister? Me? I can't imagine me as a minister! I'd be the worst minister!" I said out loud. The warmth and Light gradually filled my whole body with an exhilarating sense of well-being and peace. With an

expanding Joy in my heart, I shouted,
"OK! Ok! I'll do it! Thank you! Thank
you!"

Time passed as the stars wheeled
across the sky. I drifted in a peaceful
calm and don't remember much until
the light began to filter over the
Eastern horizon. Slowly the sun
announced its arrival with a blaze of
peach and pink bringing me to full
awareness of a new beginning of my
life. A lady and her son climbed the
hill to celebrate the dawn. We took
each other's pictures to
commemorate the moment.

I slowly walked back through the
village, hoping that I wouldn't be seen
by anyone. How could I explain that I
felt that Light was pouring out of my

eyes? I made it safely to my room with a sigh of relief.

There, on the bedside table, was the small bible. I picked it up and held it for a time. "What do you want me to know?"

I randomly opened to a page, which astonishingly said, "You have not chosen me, but I have chosen you".

I was thunderstruck by those words from the book of St. John. In shock, I totally surrendered to the idea that somehow, I would be a minister of God's Light, whatever that might mean. I knew that Life was forever changed once more, and I was awed by the magnificence of what had been given.

Fast forward several months and a phone call from my friend, therapist and meditation teacher, A.D. from New York. She said, "Since we've been hanging out with you, LiLi, we are lightening up and having more fun." She explained that she and her partner were starting a small publishing company and, "We would like you to be our Director of Fun!"

"Yes! I would be so delighted! How Fun is that? But, wait! Do you remember my story about what happened in Glastonbury? I could be a *Minister of Fun.* I think I could handle THAT. Thank you!"

I was quite enchanted with the idea. Now another beginning. Yet another!

Oz

In Santa Fe, I had met and had an immediate, deep connection with a woman named Linda Tellington Jones. She was world famous as a teacher of her technique for riding and training difficult horses, particularly ones who had been mishandled. She said, "There is no such thing as a bad horse. It is only those who have been mistreated by man. With my Tellington Touch and long-rein exercises, we can heal them and build back their trust and confidence."

I had long been entranced by the very idea of Australia and was intrigued by Linda's work and the deep bond that we had forged. I accepted an invitation to join her workshop of 16 other women, who were mostly familiar with her work. The plan was to go on a six-day camel safari near Alice Springs in the Center of Australia and watch the famous camel race across the red desert. Then we'd camp at a horse farm called Crystal Waters in the backcountry near Brisbane where they had assembled 16 horses of uncertain character.

Down Under

After several days of acclimatizing near Sydney, we flew to the Red Center of Australia. Alice Springs is a colorful frontier town surrounded by the ancient, rounded McDonnell Ranges. The quirky old buildings house many art galleries featuring the famous dot painting of Aboriginal art. With color and verve, the Dreamtime painting revealed stories that weave back into 40,000 years of continuous habitation. We were whisked off to the Virginia camel ranch, a colorful oasis in the desert where our camels awaited us. After perfunctory instructions and learning the basic commands "Whuff!" (lurch down or stand), we headed off into the arid desert, lurching along for

hours enjoying the desert flowers
and watching the dramatic sunset
unfurl with radiant reds and oranges.
The full moon rose as we rode along
to the tented encampment called
Rainbow Alley, our home base for the
next six days. With aching and
complaining thighs due to the
unaccustomed gait, we dismounted
by moonlight.

Each day brought new adventures as
we explored outlying sandstone
escarpments, dry riverbeds, glades
of eucalyptus, and swaths of purple
and yellow blooms. And best of all,
we slept under the bright canopy of
the Milky Way, cozy in our comfy
swags. (The Aussie sleeping bag
used by the swagmen immortalized in
the song, Waltzing Matilda).

We melted into Nature and Nature melted into us. We felt grounded in new ways.

Next, we drove out to Uluru, named by the colonists, Ayers Rock. The mammoth silhouette of the red stone mound looked like a giant navel – an omphalos: an 'outie' of gigantic proportions. Arriving at the base of Uluru, we were stunned at the power and beauty of the place. We circumnavigated the five-mile perimeter in an awed pilgrimage. Folds of sandstone undulated and curved as we walked and speculated at the Dreamtime stories of the Aboriginal hosts of this land. Then we began our climb up the sloping, nearly vertical ascent, which, fortunately had a strong chain of heavy iron links to assist us. About half way up, about 400 feet, the quite large sister who was ahead of me froze and gasped that she could go no further. "Nonsense, my dear," I said firmly, "you'll be just fine! I'm right here!" Thinking to myself, *Oh wow, she could squash me like a gnat!* I nudged her upwards and began to sing the Lord's Prayer. This comforted her enough to carry on to the top. This climb is no longer permitted, in respect to Aboriginal culture.

It was windy up there, overlooking the desert vastness and in the distance, a rounded ancient mountain scape called the Olgas. It looked intriguing and begged further exploration. Linda urged us to walk along the narrow undulating path until we found a pocket of flat land somewhat protected from the wind. We gathered to give thanks and meditate together.

In the silence, my inner voice clearly stated, *You are a Minister of Fun in the Church and Tribe of One, and when the time is right, we will dropkick the Church!* I was smiling to myself at this news, feeling quite enchanted. A parenthesis here to note that immediately following Alan's death, my monthly periods had stopped completely. And now, at this potent time, and with this definitive announcement, when I arose, I was flooded with blood—a powerful sign of connection with Earth Mother. It seemed to be an important and significant part of the message. "A Minister of Fun! So be it! And thanks!"

Some of us stayed in the swanky Ayer's Rock Resort and some of us camped. All of us were thrilled for the hot showers. We were looking forward, with great excitement, to the wild camel race on the following day, which took place every year, miles away from Uluru. With the spectacular sunrise in the East came the knowing feeling that I had to stay in Uluru. I was disappointed to miss the acclaimed race but determined to stay there. Six of the women were called to stay as well, and we all wandered off to be on our own. Gazing up at the flowing, rounded curves of the mount, I noticed a place where two buttresses seemed to form giant thighs of the Earth Mother. I greeted the Mother in her magnificence. As I strolled along the sandy path, words came in that I wanted to record. "Oh damn, I have paper but no pen." I walked on and a few yards later, I found a pen – and not just a Bic – it was a pricy wooden pen. It all felt so magical, and I happily sat down to write.

"Hey LiLi, come look here. We found a cave!" I heard one of my companions call out. As I approached, I could see that the shallow cave was at the apex of the great thighs that I had noticed. They urged me, as the elder, to enter first.

I knelt on a rock that was placed near the out-curving wall. "Blessed Mother Earth," I whispered, "thank you for the fierce beauty and the power of this land. May I continue to serve you in unknowable ways now and forever." Each woman entered for her own private communication, and when the last one had finished, out of my mouth, came the words, "Would you like to be ordained in the Ministry of Fun?" We stood in a semi-circle next to a tiny pool of deep green water, which seemed to us, to be the afterbirth, since we all felt reborn.

I spoke, "This is the credo of the Ministry of Fun, Raise a hand and repeat after me:

If it's not Fun,
Don't do it!
If you must do it
Make it Fun!

Each of us has
A one to one
Connection to the One!"

I had seven almonds in my pocket,
and they became the sacrament of
the Ministry of Fun.

It took twenty-five years of inner
explorations and perambulations for
the final words, which are the
completion of the ceremony:

"In truth, we are the One!"

(and, drawing an infinity sign at our third eye, this blessing:)

"Infinite Love is coming to us
Infinitely,
From the source of all Love and
Fun
Which is the same place!

Congratulations!
We are One!"

Now, nearly thirty years, and thousands of ordinations later, it all seems complete.
Of course, we know that Un-Fun may occur. When it arises, we can meet it with the infinite love and patience deep in our core. We give a sigh, and we remember the simple wisdom of

IT IS WHAT IT IS and we carry on.
Sometimes the Un-Fun brings out the
best in us!

We say that we are a global, local,
non-organization. As Ministers of
Fun, nothing will be required from
you other than to Lighten up "the
situation" into a higher level, a
frequency of awakened awareness
and opened heart.

Since there are seven billion plus
souls here on Earth, there must be
seven billion plus ways to find the
Truth. There are no two alike, and
each unique path is the correct one
for that Soul. We are all Souls-in-
Evolution working our way through
Earth School. . . . . And collectively,
we are all One!

With Loving Awareness,

LiLi
~Minister of Fun

Here's an encouraging word from
playwright Bertolt Brecht:

*"Just because things are the way they
are, doesn't mean they stay that way."*

Yes, everything is changing moment by
moment... Life is so immediately NOW!

Have FUN!
Be FUN!
Be LOVE!

P.S. ministryoffun.com is a rather pale affair
and looking for a web designer on Maui.
Contact Cara at <u>caraberry@hotmail.com</u>
if you are interested in helping

Made in the USA
San Bernardino, CA
06 September 2019